8 9 10 11 12

21 22 23 24 25 26

33 34 35 36 37 38

45 46 47 48 49 50

58 59 60 61 62 63 64

71 72 73 74 75 76

83 84 85 86 87 88

95 96 97 98 99 100

1 2 3 4 5 6 7 8 9 10 11 12 13 14 15 16 17 18 19 20 21
100   22
99   23
98   24
97   25
96   26
95   27
94   28
93   29
92   30
91   31
90   32
89   33
88   34
87   35

EMILY'S FIRST 100 DAYS OF SCHOOL

ROSEMARY WELLS

SCHOLASTIC INC.

New York Toronto London Auckland Sydney

Mexico City New Delhi Hong Kong

86   36
85   37
84   38
83   39
82   40
81   41
80   42
79   43
78   44
77   45
76   46
75   47
74   48
73   49
72   50
71 70 69 68 67 66 65 64 63 62 61 60 59 58 57 56 55 54 53 52 51

With special thanks to JoAnn Jonas, Senior Librarian,
New York Public Library Early Childhood Resource Center

ISBN 0-439-15532-0

12 11 10 9 8 7 6 5 4 3 2 1   9/9 0 1 2 3 4/0

Designed by Christine Kettner

Printed in Singapore.

First Scholastic printing

0-439-15532-0

SCHOLASTIC INC.

RL2 003-006

AUTHOR'S NOTE

WHEN I WAS LITTLE, in elementary school, math was no fun for me. It was taught by rote, and it was hard for me to see any connection between the lessons I memorized and my real-life experiences with numbers.

Yet numbers are wonderful things. They appear in all our games, in our poetry, and in songs. Numbers are a vital part of our culture. Some numbers are so much a part of our language that certain things come to mind the moment the number is mentioned; other numbers are shy and need to be brought out of their hiding places. In this book all numbers are equally important, and all are fun.

Numbers are all around us. Explore some every day with a child you love.

—*Rosemary Wells*

On the first day of school I leave my mama's arms. I am too excited to cry.

I have my own desk and my own notebook,
and my own teacher, Miss Cribbage.

Miss Cribbage says, "Every morning we will make a new number
friend and write it down in our number books. When we reach one
hundred days we will have a big party." No one believes we will ever
get to one hundred days.

On the second day of school Miss Cribbage teaches us a song
called "Tea for Two." Two is our number friend for the day.
I write it in my journal and on the way home I sing "Tea for Two."

My school bus is the number three bus.
Papa makes sure I know the number three so
that after school I get on the right school bus.

My partner in square dancing is Diane Duck. There are four corners to a dancing square.

After school I pick five different vegetables in our garden. Papa makes tomato-zucchini-pepper-carrot-eggplant soup.

We eat supper at six o'clock. I draw a clock with the hands at six for my number journal.

7

🌼 he loves me

🌼 he loves me not

🌼 he loves me

My big sister, Eloise, has a daisy with seven petals. "He loves me, he loves me not, he loves me, he loves me not, he loves me," says Eloise.
"WHO?" I ask. But Eloise won't tell.

8

My little brother, Leo, has a cold and stays in bed all day. After school I teach him Crazy Eights.

9

Miss Cribbage shows us a map of the night sky.
There are nine planets in our solar system.
I come as Saturn.

Mercury

Venus

Earth

Mars

Jupiter

Saturn

Uranus

Neptune

Pluto

Miss Cribbage comes as the sun. "Nine planets plus one sun is ten heavenly bodies," says Miss Cribbage.

Every day at quiet time we read a different picture book. We copy the names of the books on paper leaves and pin the leaves to a tree. My book tree has eleven leaves.

Leo and I pick Mama a dozen zinnias for her birthday surprise. "Who could have done such a wonderful thing!" Mama said.

Eloise is thirteen years old. She thinks she knows everything.

Miss Cribbage gives us all gold stars for writing our names without any mistakes. I write *Emily* in fourteen different colors.

15

My best friend in school is Diane Duck. Her daddy takes us for a boat ride. His motor is fifteen horsepower.
"Is that like fifteen horses swimming?" I ask.

16

You load

Six-teen Tons, what do you get?—

After supper Leo, Eloise, Granny, Grandpa, and I sing "Sixteen Tons."

Miss Cribbage reads aloud
Dick and the Donkey.
I follow along and read
seventeen of the words all
by myself.
"Wow!" says Miss Cribbage.

Mrs. Como is blind. Diane Duck and I walk with her across
Main Street. "Eighteen steps from sidewalk
to sidewalk!" says Mrs. Como.
"I know where I am."

Leo eats pineapple upside-down
cake upside down. My mama says,
"You can make pineapple upside-
down cake ninteen ways but only
eat it one way."

20

We bring big cardboard cartons in to school.
Miss Cribbage makes three of them into isolation booths.
Then we play Twenty Questions.

ANIMAL

VEGETABLE

MINERAL

21

Today is our music teacher's birthday.
The class sings, "Happy birthday,
Mr. Horne!" and gives him a
twenty-one-horn salute.

22

Grandpa takes us to a football game.
I count eleven players on each side.
Grandpa helps. Twenty-two footballers
altogether.

23

Our seats are in
section twenty-three
of the grandstand.

Today each family in our class bakes two dozen cookies.

They bring them in for open house night at school.

I draw all twenty-four cookies in my journal.

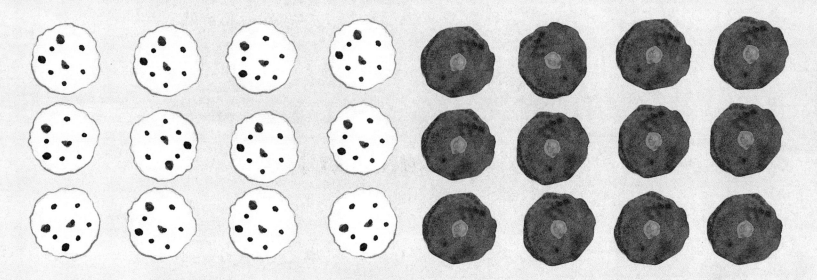

25

I collect twenty-five Japanese beetles from the garden. I get a penny for each one. Twenty-five pennies make a quarter.

26

There are twenty-six
letters in the alphabet
and I can write them all.
Capital and uncapital.

NORTH
PLEASANT VALLEY
BY - THE - SEA

I read a road sign for our hometown,
North Pleasant Valley by-the-Sea.
That's a twenty-seven-letter name!

27

28

"Don't you want to eat your
vegetable Jell-O?" asks our school lunch monitor.
"I'm counting the peas in it first," I answer.
There are twenty-eight peas in my Jell-O cup.

29

Today a new boy moves to
our school. His name is
Roger and he comes from
Twenty-nine Palms,
California. We look it up
on the map.

September

Sun	Mon	Tues	Wed	Thor	Fri	Sat
					1	2
3	4	5	6	7	8	9
10	11	12	13	14	15	16
17	18	19	20	21	22	23
24	25	26	27	28	29	30

30

Miss Cribbage teaches us to recite a poem.

Thirty days has September,
April, June, and November.
All the rest have thirty-one,
Except February, now we're done.

31

October

Sun	Mon.	Tues.	Wed.	Thur	Fri	Sat
1	2	3	4	5	6	7
8	9	10	11	12	13	14
15	16	17	18	19	20	21
22	23	24	25	26	27	28
29	30	31				

Eloise has thirty-two Girl Scout merit badges including First Aid. When Leo falls out of the tree, she makes him a sling from her tie.

The prizewinning pumpkin at the state fair weighs thirty-three pounds.

Last night's wind blew acorns on to our front steps. I count thirty-four and make a necklace for Granny.

Miss Cribbage has a letter from her brother in Costa Rica. The stamp says thirty-five *centivos*. "Someday I'll write a letter all the way to Costa Rica!" I tell Miss Cribbage.

Eloise, Leo, and I make growing marks in ink on our kitchen wall. We measure with a yardstick, which is thirty-six inches long.

Eloise shows me the number thirty-seven in her homework. "It's a prime number," says Eloise. "Nothing goes into it. Someday you'll understand." Eloise always says things like that.

38

Our neighbor Mr. Huffington drives a very old car. "It's a thirty-eight DeSoto," says Mr. Huffington. "Best car ever made."

1938

39

"I'm four. How old are you, Aunt Min?" Leo asks. "I am thirty-nine years old," answers Aunt Min. "Still a spring chicken."

40

Daddy makes Leo a Noah's ark for his birthday. "The real Noah's ark sailed for forty days and forty nights!" Dad says. After Leo's birthday party Dad takes forty winks on the sofa.

Diane Duck visits New York City. The airline loses forty-one pieces of luggage on Diane's flight. Her mother has to get Diane new clothes.

42

Diane sends the class a postcard from New York City with a picture of Forty-second Street. I get to read it aloud to the whole class during circle time.

43

Leo is an astronaut for Halloween. Grandpa makes Leo a space helmet with forty-three fiber-optic meteor-proof antennae on it.

It is Rain Forest Day. Miss Cribbage shows us a picture of a square foot of Amazon jungle.

"How many beetles can you count?" Miss Cribbage asks.

I count forty-four.

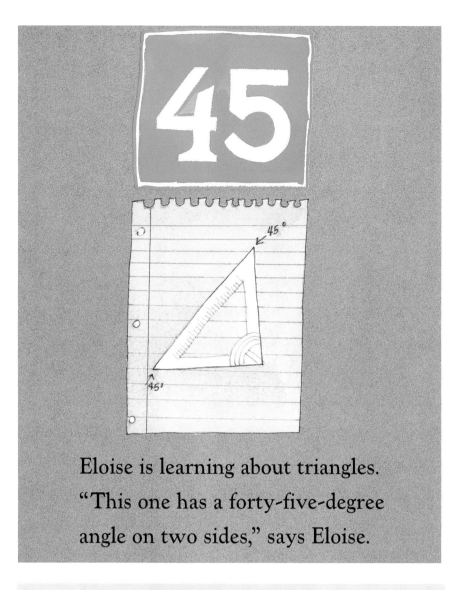

Eloise is learning about triangles. "This one has a forty-five-degree angle on two sides," says Eloise.

The sixth grade boys play the girls in basketball. The score is forty-six to forty-six. Our class are the cheerleaders.

At circle time I read a whole book out loud. It has forty-seven words to it.

Felix eats four twelve-packs of candy corn from Halloween. The school nurse sends him home with his mama. That's forty-eight candy corns.

49

"Clementine" is my papa's favorite song in the shower. "What's a miner forty-niner?" I ask him. "Someone who went west for gold back in 1849," he tells me.

In a cav-ern, in a can-yon, Ex-ca-va-ting for a mine, Dwelt a

50

Every day we salute our flag. There are fifty stars on it, one for each state. We make a map of the states in our number journals.

51

My sister, Eloise, thinks she is so grown-up, but she is not allowed to go into the big city with her friends. "There are fifty-one reasons why not," says our papa. Eloise does not stay put to hear them.

52

Diane Duck has moved away and I am so sad.
Granny plays Hearts with me to make me feel
better. There are fifty-two cards in the deck
and I know each one.

"Write Diane Duck a long letter with lots of pictures," says my mama. And we do. I make the pictures and Mama writes my words down. We address it to her new house at Fifty-three Buckaroo Boulevard in Pecos, New Mexico.

The geese fly over us heading south for the winter. I mark off fifty-four Goose dots on Miss Cribbage's nature chart.

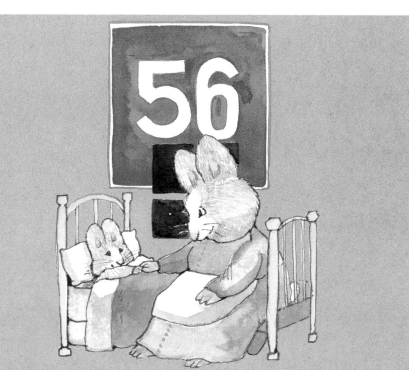

"Why can't we zoom like the motorcycles?" Leo asks my Papa.
"Because the speed limit is fifty-five miles per hour," says my papa.

"How Do I Love Thee? Let Me Count the Ways" is Mama's favorite poem.
"How many ways are there?" I ask.
"Off the top of my head I can count Fifty-six ways," says Mama.

We make piccalilli for class Thanksgiving. The label on our
pickle jar says FIFTY-SEVEN VARIETIES on it.
"What are the names of the fifty-seven kinds of pickles?" I ask.
But even Miss Cribbage doesn't know.

58

Granny and I take the pies out to cool on Thanksgiving Day. But it is fifty-eight degrees outside. "Indian summer," Granny calls it.

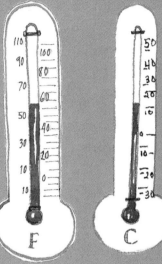

59

At Thanksgiving dinner everyone says thanks for one thing. Leo says thanks for all fifty-nine cranberries in the cranberry sauce.

60

I watch the timer for Mama while she cooks. There are sixty minutes in each hour.

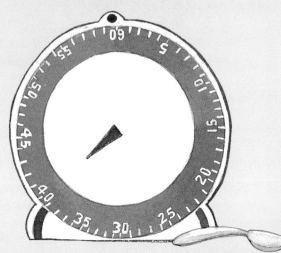

Everyone in our class makes
turkey sandwiches for the homeless
people so they have Thanksgiving, too. We make five dozen plus one for Dorothy,
who drives the truck. That's sixty-one sandwiches altogether.

Papa and I do the weekly shopping.
There are sixty-two things on Mama's list.

"Hello! Good morning!" says everyone on the school bus.
I counted sixty-three hellos.

"Why is the sky blue?" Felix asks Granny. "That's the sixty-four-thousand-dollar question," says Granny.

Louise is our class track star.
She can run the one hundred meter dash in sixty-five seconds.

"What will we do when we grow up?" Miss Cribbage asks the class. "I'll drive my very own car all the way along Route Sixty-six right across America. And I'll visit Diane Duck on the way," I answer.

Diane Duck sends me mail! It's my first package ever. It has my name and SIXTY-SEVEN OAK STREET right on the envelope. In the package is a tumbleweed.

68

Grandpa brings home sixty-eight tulip bulbs.
They will flower next spring. We plant some in
Mr. Kerensky's garden because he is too old to
plant anymore.

69

Eloise plays a duet with Clara for the Girl Scout holiday concert. They have learned "Opus Sixty-nine" of Mozart. "That means the sixty-ninth thing Mozart wrote," says Eloise.

70

Everyone in the lower school lights tiny Hanukkah candles in the cafeteria. Seventy candles make a beautiful light.

71

Granny and I love to bake. First we measure carefully. "Two scoops of chocolate drops!" says Granny.

"That's seventy-one grams!" say I.

72

Altogether we make six dozen Christmas, Hanukkah, Kwanza, and solstice cookies for the children in the children's hospital.

73

Eloise and I make six dozen (plus one for Miss Cribbage's dachshund, Binky) rice-and-egg biscuits for the animal shelter's Christmas dinner.

74 inches of snow in the Rockies

"It will be a white Christmas!" says Miss Cribbage.
She draws us a weather map on the blackboard.
We color it in. "Seventy-four inches of snow fell in the Rocky Mountains,"
says Miss Cribbage. "Think of that!"

75

Grandpa is building a clipper ship out of
matchsticks. He keeps a seventy-five-watt
bulb in his work light.

Eloise has been asked to play "Seventy-six Trombones"
for the Girl Scout jamboree.
"Do you have to practice seventy-six times a day?"
asks Papa.

Sev - en - ty Six Trom - bones led the big pa - rade,—

— With a hun-dred and ten cor - nets close at hand.—

Everyone makes a Christmas stocking for the UNICEF
Christmas Crusade. Our school sends stockings to seventy-seven
children in different countries around the world. I want to write
a letter to whoever gets my stocking in a faraway land. I can't
write all of the words so I put down:

Happy Happy Happy 🎄!

78

We string Christmas tree chains. Miss Cribbage dunks them in gold and silver paint. Mine has seventy-eight pieces of silver-painted popcorn.

79

"What's another word for snowstorm?" asks Mama.

"Blizzard!" I say. Mama shows me how to spell *blizzard* and lets me write it in her crossword puzzle under seventy-nine down.

Angela is a new girl in school. She comes all the way from Eighty-Mile Beach in Australia.

Angela tells us about Ayers Rock, kangaroos, platypuses and eucalyptus trees.

Then we find Australia on the map.

81

Miss Cribbage is teaching us about great buildings of the world. I make an Egyptian pyramid out of eighty-one sugar cubes. Leo eats the top cube in the car.

82

Angela needs friends. My mama asks Angela's whole family to come for supper. Angela and I skip rope double dutch eighty-two times without stopping.

83 TROOP 83

Angela's big sister, Freida, is a Girl Guide. Eloise invites her to join troop eighty-three of the Girl Scouts of America. Freida says yes and wears her Australian uniform.

84

We make seven dozen cookies for the firemen's ball.
Angela dances to the fireman's fiddle.

85

Our gym teacher does eighty-five jumping jacks every morning.

86

The tallest building in our state capitol is eighty-six steps high to the top of the dome. Our class walks up all the way and down all the way.

Angela stays overnight. She is now my best friend. We count eighty-seven stars in the sky. My mama says Australian stars are all different, but the moon is the same.

Every Tuesday at lunchtime I sit with Mr. Horne at his piano. There are eighty-eight keys on the piano and Mr. Horne plays them all. I can play and read three notes.

Aunt Mim is on a diet. "There are only eighty-nine calories in my tomato soup," says Aunt Mim.

"I can't see any," says Leo.

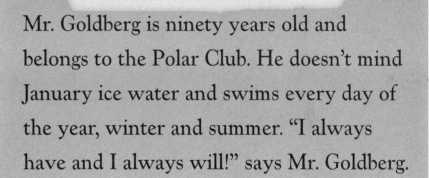

Mr. Goldberg is ninety years old and belongs to the Polar Club. He doesn't mind January ice water and swims every day of the year, winter and summer. "I always have and I always will!" says Mr. Goldberg.

Miss Cribbage tells us her dachshund, Binky, is really an old lady of ninety-one years. (That's thirteen dog years old.)

I turn the radio dial to my favorite station, Country Ninety-two, the banjo music station.

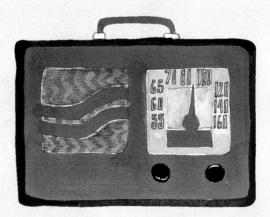

93

Angela has never seen ice before, so we take her skating. My papa lets us measure the ice through an ice fisherman's hole. The ice is ninety-three centimeters thick on the pond and that's plenty safe.

A storm knocks down one of our trees.
"We'll read the trunk to find out how old
the tree was," says my Grandpa. There are
ninety-four rings in the slice of tree.
One for each year.

"I have ninety-five things to do," says
my papa. "But the most important thing is
reading you your story."

We make eight dozen
gingerbread policemen
with gold marshmallow
buttons for the
policemen's jamboree.
The policemen eat
every single one.

It's Clean Up Our Neighborhood Day!
Our class wins the blue ribbon for picking up
ninety-seven bottles and cans.

98

I have the sniffles. Mama takes my temperature. "Ninety-eight degrees is normal!" says Mama, but she brings me hot chocolate and lets me stay home from school anyway. In bed I write to Diane Duck. This time my letter is more words than pictures.

99

On my school bus everyone sings. Today we sing "Ninety-nine Bottles of Pop on the Wall."

Suddenly it is the hundredth day of school.
"I can think of a hundred new things to do!" says Miss Cribbage.

Felix brings in a
hundred candy corns.

Martha wears a hundred buttons.

Otto plays a hundred
rat-tat-tat-tats.

Roger stands on one foot
for one hundred seconds.

Angela recites a
hundred-word poem.

Terrance does a
hundred cartwheels.

Lewis makes a glued-together
hundred-bottle-cap hat.

Louise runs a hundred yards.

"What are you going to do, Emily?"
asks everyone.
But my hundred is a secret.

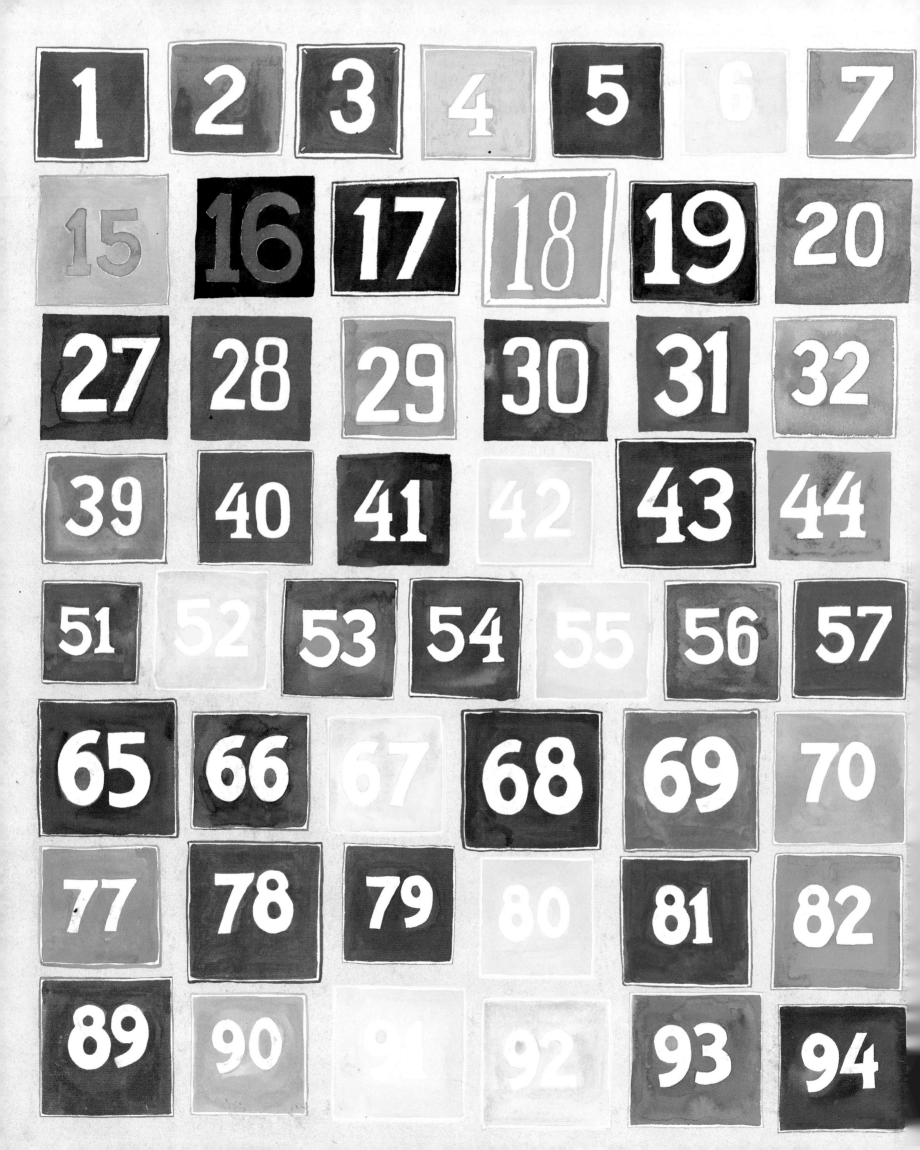